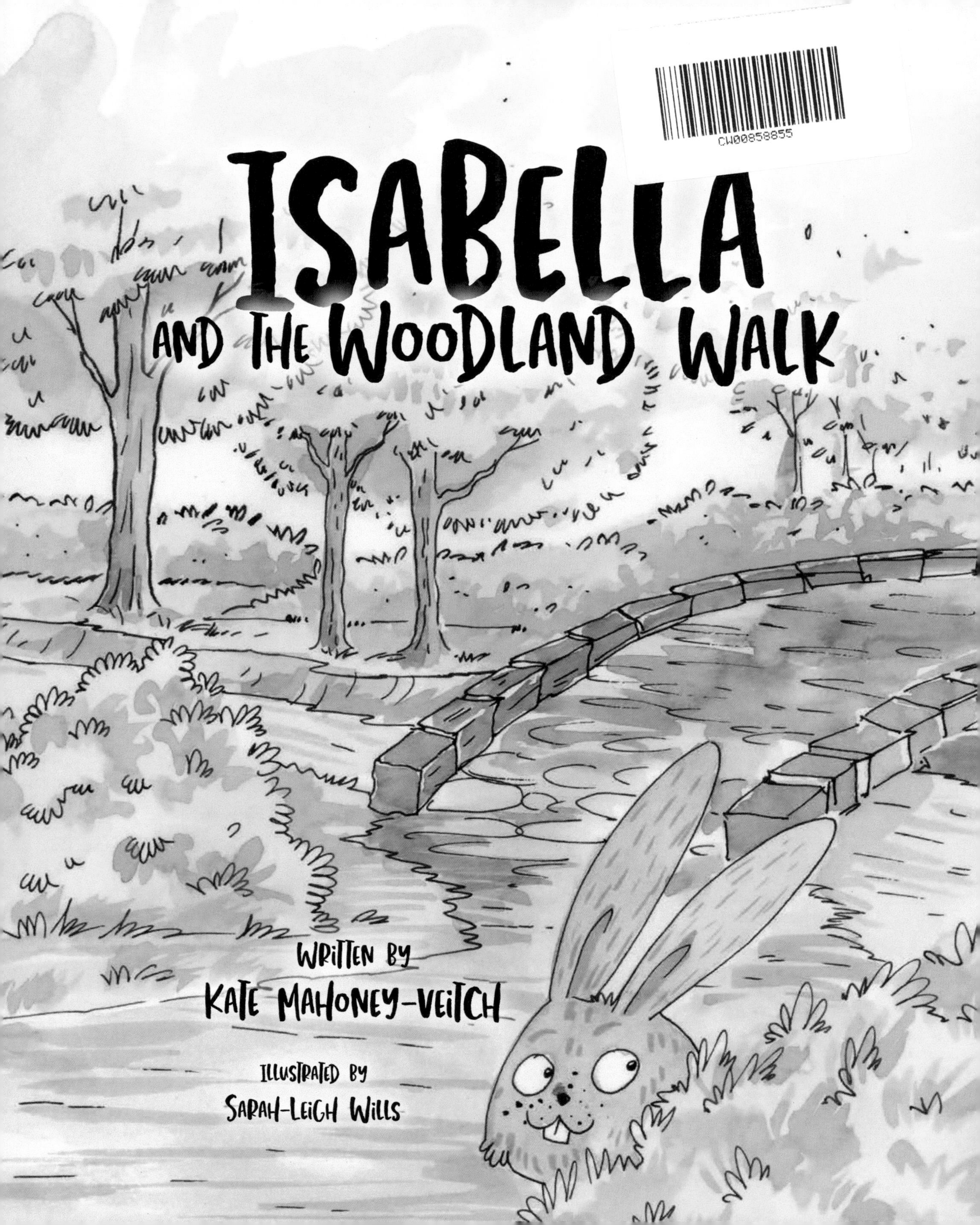
CW00858855
ISABELLA
AND THE WOODLAND WALK
WRITTEN BY
KATE MAHONEY-VEITCH
ILLUSTRATED BY
SARAH-LEIGH WILLS

For my Daddy, for always listening without judging and believing in my dreams.

Isabella and the Woodland Walk

Illustration and design by Sarah-Leigh Wills.
www.happydesigner.co.uk

Isabella is a little girl who loves soft toys; she has so many of them that they take up most of her bed, the window sills in her bedroom, on top of her wardrobe and bookshelves. She loves them all, but her favourites are Monkey Snuggles, Snuggly Rabbit, Jessie the Cat, Daddy Leopard, Baby Leopard and Duke the Pup.

Isabella also absolutely loves books, she has lots of them; three bookshelves full in fact! She loves looking at the pictures and telling magical stories to her soft toys.

Animal
Stories

Today Isabella is taking her dog, Dukie, for a walk in the woods with her Mummy, her Grandad, her little brother Vinnie and her favourite soft toys.

They walk over a small bridge and Mummy says in a deep voice: "Who's this trip-trapping over my bridge?" Isabella laughs and runs over the bridge as fast as she can. Dukie runs past as fast as a rocket as he's seen a rabbit ahead; he absolutely loves the woods.

Isabella spots a statue of a squirrel so they walk over and pretend to feed him some acorns. They come to a clearing where a tree has fallen down. Isabella gathers her soft toys and sits down to tell them an exciting story.

"One day a little girl called Isabella and her best friends go for a walk in the woods. They are very excited; they run along the stream, they climb trees and they play hide and seek!"

"But the fun stops when they can't find Duke the Pup. Isabella is very worried; she calls and calls for him but he does not return."

"Monkey climbs a tree to see if he can spot
Duke the Pup but he gets stuck in the branches.
"Oooo ooooo, aaaah aaah!" he cries."

"Rabbit is too scared to go over the bridge
so Daddy Leopard puts her on his back and
runs over quickly to see if they can find him."

"But it is no good, they can't find him anywhere! They all shout: "Duke, come!" Finally Duke the Pup skulks back, all stinky and covered in mud. He's looking very sorry for himself. "I was chasing a rabbit and I got stuck in the mud," he whimpered."

"Isabella gives him a small pat on the head, she doesn't want to get dirty too, and says to all her friends, "It is very important to stay together and not run off, otherwise next time someone could get very lost and very stuck."

Grandad walks over with Dukie close behind. "Time to go, Isabella," he says, smiling.

Isabella gathers up her soft toys, takes Grandad's hand, and skips away happily.

THE ISABELLA SERIES...

Isabella is a little girl who adores soft toys and books. She loves making up magical stories where her soft toys come to life and have exciting adventures with her.

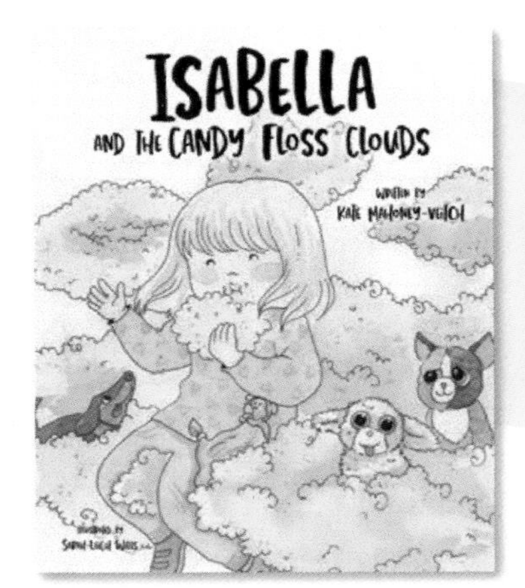

ISABELLA AND THE CANDY FLOSS CLOUDS

In this story Isabella and her soft toys wake up in clouds made of candy floss and discover a sticky world of shapes.

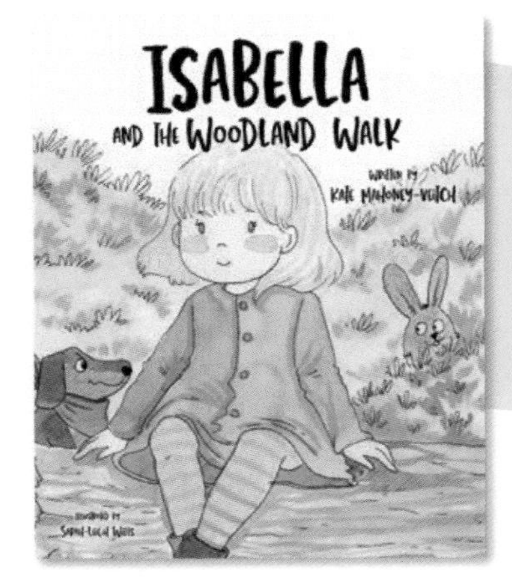

ISABELLA AND THE WOODLAND WALK

In this story Isabella goes for a woodland walk with her soft toys but one of them gets lost!

ISABELLA AT GYMNASTICS

In this story Isabella and her soft toys all go to gymnastics and turn a bit wild!

ISABELLA AT THE LIBRARY

In this story Isabella and her soft toys go to the library where they visit the world of nursery rhymes.

ISABELLA AND THE MAGIC UMBRELLA

In this story Isabella and her soft toys discover that they have a magic umbrella.

38260803R00019

Printed in Poland
by Amazon Fulfillment
Poland Sp. z o.o., Wrocław